The best det

For nearly a whole y... escaped arrest and no b... with breaking a single law in Idaville.

This was partly because the town's police-men were clever and brave. But mostly it was because Chief Brown was Encyclopedia's father.

His hardest cases were solved by Encyclopedia during dinner in the Browns' red brick house on Rover Avenue.

Everyone in the state thought that Idaville had about the smartest policemen in the world.

Of course, nobody knew a boy was the mastermind behind the town's police force.

Read all the books in the Encyclopedia Brown series!

Encyclopedia Brown
and His
Best Cases Ever

BY DONALD J. SOBOL

illustrated by
James Bernardin
Lillian Brandi
Leonard Shortall

PUFFIN BOOKS
An Imprint of Penguin Group (USA)

PUFFIN BOOKS
Published by the Penguin Group
Penguin Group (USA) LLC
375 Hudson Street
New York, New York 10014

USA * Canada * UK * Ireland * Australia
New Zealand * India * South Africa * China

penguin.com
A Penguin Random House Company

Published by Puffin Books, a member of Penguin Young Readers Group, 2013

The Case of Natty Nat and The Case of Merko's Grandson
previously published in *Encyclopedia Brown, Boy Detective*, 1963

The Case of the Secret Pitch
previously published in *Encyclopedia Brown and The Case of the Secret Pitch*, 1965

The Case of the Stolen Diamonds
previously published in *Encyclopedia Brown Finds the Clues*, 1966

The Case of the Explorer's Money
previously published in *Encyclopedia Brown Gets His Man*, 1967

The Case of the Super-Secret Hold and The Case of the Muscle Maker
previously published in *Encyclopedia Brown Solves Them All*, 1968

The Case of the Junk Sculptor
previously published in *Encyclopedia Brown Saves the Day*, 1970

The Case of the Champion Skier
previously published in *Encyclopedia Brown Tracks Them Down*, 1971

The Case of the Stolen Money
previously published in *Encyclopedia Brown Takes the Case*, 1973

The Case of the Skunk Ape
previously published in *Encyclopedia Brown Lends a Hand*, 1974

The Case of the Dead Eagles
previously published in *Encyclopedia Brown and the Case of the Dead Eagles*, 1975

The Case of the Hit-Run Car
previously published in *Encyclopedia Brown and the Case of the Midnight Visitor*, 1977

The Case of the Gym Bag
previously published in *Encyclopedia Brown, Super Sleuth*, 2009

The Case of Mrs. Washington's Diary
previously published in *Encyclopedia Brown and the Case of the Secret UFOs*, 2010

CIP data is available

Puffin Books ISBN 978-0-14-750871-3

Printed in the United States of America

13 15 17 19 20 18 16 14 12

CONTENTS

How Encyclopedia Brown Started

Most of us have been told what date we were born and where we were born—in the hospital, on the way to the hospital, at home, or somewhere. For Encyclopedia Brown, the start was a little different. He was born over several years. But I remember vividly the day that it all began in the most fitting of places a fictional character in a book could be born. It was in a magnificent marble and brick building in the heart of New York City that stands on a two-block section of Fifth Avenue between Fortieth and Forty-second streets—the New York Public Library, whose opening ceremony in 1911 was presided over by no less a personage than William Howard Taft, president of the United States.

I did my research there in the 1950s. On one particular occasion I requested four books that had to be retrieved from underground within the stacks that held the library's massive collection.

After a brief wait, the books appeared. Three were ones I had requested, but the fourth was not. It was a mistake, but it was the best mistake that would ever happen to me. To say it changed my life would not be an overstatement.

The fourth book, filled with puzzles, had a curious layout with questions printed on the front side of a page and the solutions on the back side. I decided to try my hand at a few of them and had just flunked out on the third straight puzzle when it hit me. Why not a mystery column of no more than 150- to 300-word mysteries, with the solutions printed on a separate page? For added appeal, have the same detective solve all the mysteries. Wow!

That day I left the library as though stepping to the beat of "The Stars and Stripes Forever."

Samples of the column were written and sold, and the column was syndicated to newspapers. The column was called "Two-Minute Mysteries" and was in print in the United States and abroad for seven years before being retired. The stories, aimed at an adult audience, were collected and published in three small paperback books that are still in print today.

The mysteries led to a conversation that sparked an idea for a new book. This time, the main character would be a boy detective. I needed a good name, one that would instantly convey this was a book about a boy whiz. I quickly decided on Encyclopedia. A short second name was essential, so the reader wouldn't be put off. Brown seemed to go best with Encyclopedia, better than Smith or Jones or half a dozen other simple names. As for his given name, Leroy, well I just liked that name for some reason and thought it sounded right.

I wanted Encyclopedia to be the boy next door, believable and well liked. Whether on or off a case he is neither a braggart nor a snob and always stands ready to help others. He is not greedy either. His fee doesn't break the piggy bank and can be dug out of any kid's pocket— twenty-five cents. On special occasions he does not charge at all. He sets an example by a life of honesty and caring. I wanted to write more than one book and decided right from the start that Encyclopedia would forever be ten years old. This way, a reader could start with any book in the series rather than having to start with the first one.

I knew that I needed simply to give Encyclopedia a good mystery to solve, provide my younger readers with clues, and give them an honest chance to match wits with him. I figured that would be more than enough to hold their interest. The only violence in the stories comes in the form of an occasional fistfight, which I allowed because Encyclopedia opposes violence to solve problems and does not engage in fights. The reader may take this as a character flaw, but every character needs to have at least one flaw to help make him believable and this one seemed to fit.

The truth is, nowhere is it written that Encyclopedia fears to fight. He simply lets Sally Kimball, the junior partner in his Brown Detective Agency, volunteer to handle the rough stuff. Sally is willing to punch out the guilty boys and girls who want to punch out Encyclopedia. The culprits typically end up with a mouthful of grass, regretting the error of their ways. The series began in a different era, and a young girl who was smart and physically protected her detective friend was rather extraordinary for the time. Judging from the fan mail, Sally quickly became the readers' favorite character after Encyclopedia.

Close behind her in popularity rank two frequent members of the cast: Bugs Meany, the undaunted bully, and Wilford Wiggins, the fast-talking con artist.

Encyclopedia's detecting was fun to write. His books are relieved of lessons and messages, as none were needed. I thought I had a winner. Was I in for a surprise.

The manuscript for the first Encyclopedia book, *Encyclopedia Brown, Boy Detective*, was done in 1961. Apparently, there were many who did not believe in Encyclopedia as much as I did. Rejections from publishers began to mount up. A total of twenty-four publishers in all rejected the manuscript. But my belief in Encyclopedia never wavered, and I persevered.

Finally I found a publisher willing to take a chance on a ten-year-old boy. After two long years, the first book reached bookstores in 1963, half a century ago. Now Encyclopedia Brown would have his chance to step into the sunlight. Little did I know then he would still be going strong on his fiftieth birthday, with twenty-eight titles in the series. The appearance of each new book brings a run of extra fan mail from young readers all over the world. While every letter from young or old is precious, perhaps the most inspiring ones are from grateful parents and teachers saying that Encyclopedia has converted a reluctant reader to an avid one.

I'm grateful for all the letters, just as I am grateful to Encyclopedia Brown, whom I believe in as much today as I did during his first case. He is a remarkable young boy. Who could disagree? He's the only ten-year-old I know celebrating his fiftieth birthday.

Donald J. Sobol
April 2012

For my daughter-in-law Jodi Sobol
and my grandson Nicholas Rich.
You both brought us the greatest joy.

The Case of Natty Nat

Mr. and Mrs. Brown had one child. They called him Leroy, and so did his teachers.

Everyone else in Idaville called him Encyclopedia.

An encyclopedia is a book or a set of books giving information, arranged alphabetically, on all branches of knowledge.

Leroy Brown's head was like an encyclopedia. It was filled with facts he had learned from books. He was like a complete library walking around in sneakers.

Old ladies who did crossword puzzles were always stopping him on the street to ask him questions.

Just last Sunday, after church, Mrs. Conway, the butcher's wife, had asked him: "What is a three-letter word for a Swiss river beginning with A?"

"Aar," Encyclopedia answered after a moment.

He always waited a moment. He wanted to be helpful. But he was afraid that people might not like him if he answered their questions too quickly and sounded *too* smart.

His father asked him more questions than anyone else. Mr. Brown was the chief of police of Idaville.

The town had four banks, three movie theaters, and a Little League. It had the usual number of gasoline stations, churches, schools, stores, and comfortable houses on shady streets. It even had a mansion or two, and some dingy sections. And it had the average number of crimes for a community of its size.

Idaville, however, only *looked* like the usual American town. It was, really, most *un*usual.

For nearly a whole year no criminal had escaped arrest and no boy or girl had got away with breaking a single law in Idaville.

This was partly because the town's policemen were clever and brave. But mostly it was because Chief Brown was Encyclopedia's father.

His hardest cases were solved by Encyclopedia during dinner in the Browns' red brick house on Rover Avenue.

Everyone in the state thought that Idaville had about the smartest policemen in the world.

Of course, nobody knew a boy was the mastermind behind the town's police force.

You wouldn't guess it by looking at Encyclopedia. He looked like almost any fifth-grade boy and acted like one, too—except that he never talked about himself.

Mr. Brown never said a word about the advice his son gave him. Who would believe that his best detective was only ten years old?

This is how it began:

One evening at dinner, Mr. Brown said,

"Natty Nat has struck again. He has held up another store—and right here in Idaville."

"What store, Dad?" asked Encyclopedia.

"The Men's Shop, owned by Mr. Dillon and Mr. Jones," answered Mr. Brown. "That makes six stores Natty Nat has held up in the state this month."

"Are you sure the robber was Natty Nat?" asked Encyclopedia.

"Mr. Dillon himself said it was Natty Nat," replied Mr. Brown.

He pulled a notebook from his pocket and put it beside his plate. "I wrote down everything Mr. Dillon told me about the holdup. I'll read it to you."

Encyclopedia closed his eyes. He always closed his eyes when he was getting ready to think hard.

His father began to read what Mr. Dillon, the storekeeper, had told him about the holdup:

I was alone in the store. I did not know anyone had come in. Suddenly a man's voice told me to raise my hands. I looked up then. I was face to face with the man the newspapers call Natty Nat. He had on a gray coat with a belt in the back, just as the newspapers said. He told me to turn and face the wall. Since he had a gun, I did as he said. When I turned around again, he was gone—with all the money.

Chief Brown finished reading and closed his notebook.

Encyclopedia asked only one question: "Did the newspapers ever print a picture of Natty Nat?"

"No," answered his father. "He never stands still long enough for a picture to be taken. Remember, he's never been caught. But every policeman in the state knows he always wears that gray coat with the belt in the back."

"Nobody even knows his real name," said Encyclopedia, half to himself. "Natty Nat is just what the newspapers call him."

Suddenly he opened his eyes. "Say, the only reason Mr. Dillon thought it was Natty Nat was because of that gray coat!" he said. "The case is solved!"

"There is nothing to solve," objected Chief Brown. "There is no mystery. Mr. Dillon was robbed. The holdup man was the same one who has been robbing other stores in the state."

"Not quite," said Encyclopedia. "There was no holdup at The Men's Shop."

"What do you mean?" exclaimed Mr. Brown.

"I mean Mr. Dillon wasn't robbed, Dad. He lied from beginning to end," answered Encyclopedia.

"Why should Mr. Dillon lie?" demanded his father.

"I guess he spent the money. He didn't want his partner, Mr. Jones, to know it was missing," said Encyclopedia. "So Mr. Dillon said he was robbed."

"Leroy," said his mother, "please explain what you are saying."

"It's simple, Mom," said Encyclopedia. "Mr. Dillon read all about Natty Nat in the news-

"Go on, Leroy," said Mr. Brown.

papers. So he knew Natty Nat always wore a gray coat with a belt in the back when he held up stores."

"Go on, Leroy," said Mr. Brown, leaning forward.

"Mr. Dillon knew it would sound much better if he could blame his holdup on someone people have read about," said Encyclopedia. "He said he knew it was Natty Nat because of the coat he wore—"

"That could be true," Chief Brown said.

"That *couldn't* be true," said Encyclopedia. "Mr. Dillon never saw the back of the man who held him up. He said so himself. Remember?"

Chief Brown frowned. He picked up his notebook again. He read to himself a while.

Then he fairly shouted, "Leroy, I believe you are right!"

Encyclopedia said, "Mr. Dillon only saw the *front* of the holdup man. He had no way of knowing that the man's coat had a belt *in the back!*"

"He stole money from his own store and from his partner too," cried Chief Brown. "And he nearly got away with it!"

He rushed from the dining room.

"Leroy," said Mrs. Brown, "did you get this idea from a television program?"

"No," said Encyclopedia. "I got it from a book I read about a great detective and his methods of observation."

"Well," said his mother proudly, "this proves how important it is to listen carefully and watch closely, to train your memory. Perhaps *you* will be a detective when you grow up."

"Mom," said Encyclopedia, "can I have another piece of pie?"

Mrs. Brown sighed. She had taught English in the Idaville High School before her marriage. "You *may* have another piece of pie," she said.

The Case of Merko's Grandson

Bugs Meany and his Tigers liked to spend rainy afternoons in their clubhouse. Usually, they sat around thinking up ways of getting even with Encyclopedia Brown.

But today they had met for another purpose—to cheer the boy detective on.

Encyclopedia and Sally Kimball were about to meet in a battle of brains.

The Tigers hated Sally even more than they hated Encyclopedia—and with good reason.

When Sally had moved into the neighborhood two months ago, the Tigers jumped to show off for her. She was very pretty and she was very good at sports.

In fact, she got up a team of fifth-grade girls and challenged the Tigers to a game of softball. The boys thought it was a big joke, till Sally started striking them out. She was the whole team. In the last inning she hit the home run that won for the girls, 1–0.

But the real blow fell on the Tigers the next day.

Bugs was bullying a small boy when Sally happened to ride by on her bicycle.

"Let him go!" she ordered, hopping to the ground.

Bugs snarled. The snarl changed to a gasp as Sally broke his grip on the boy.

Before the other Tigers knew what to do, Sally had knocked their leader down with a quick left to the jaw.

Bugs bounced up, surprised and angry. He pushed Sally. She hit him again, with a right to the jaw. Bugs said *oooh*, and went down again.

For the next thirty seconds Bugs bounced up and down like a beach ball. By the fourth bounce, he was getting up a lot more slowly than he was going down.

"I'm going to make you sorry," he said. But his voice was weak, and he wore the sick smile of a boy who had taken one ride too many on a roller coaster.

"So?" said Sally. She moved her feet and took careful aim.

"This," she said, aiming another blow, "should take the frosting off you."

Bugs landed on his back, flat as a fifteen-cent sandwich. Not until Sally had ridden away did he dare get up.

Sally was not content to rest on her victories at softball and fighting. She aimed higher.

She set out to prove she was not only stronger than any boy up to twelve years of age in Idaville, but smarter, too!

That meant out-thinking the thinking machine, Encyclopedia Brown.

The great battle of brains took place in the

Tigers' clubhouse. The two champions, seated on orange crates, faced each other. The Tigers crowded behind Encyclopedia. The girls' softball team crowded behind Sally. That left just enough room in the tool shed to think.

Everyone stopped talking when Peter Clinton, the referee, announced the rules.

"Sally has five minutes to tell a mystery. She must give all the clues. Then Encyclopedia will have five minutes to solve the mystery. Ready, you two?"

"Ready," said the girl champion.

"Ready," said Encyclopedia, closing his eyes.

"Go!" called Peter, eyes on his watch.

Sally began to tell the story:

"The Great Merko was the best trapeze artist the world had ever seen. People in every big city were thrilled by the wonderful performer swinging fifty feet above the ground!

"In the year 1922, Merko died at the very height of fame. In Merko's desk was found a letter. It was a will, written by the circus star. The will directed that the star's money be put in a bank for forty years.

"After forty years, the money was to be taken out and given to Merko's oldest grandson. If no grandson was alive, all the money was to go to Merko's nearest relative, man or woman.

"Forty years passed. A search was begun. At last a man was found in Kansas City who said he was Merko's grandson. His name was Fred Gibson. He went to court to claim his inheritance.

"While the judge was listening to him, a tall woman in the back of the courtroom jumped up. She was very excited.

"The woman said she was the trapeze artist's grandniece. She kept shouting that the Great Merko was not Fred Gibson's grandfather. Therefore, the money was rightfully hers.

"The judge questioned the woman. He had to agree with what she said. She was Merko's grandniece, and the Great Merko was *not* Fred Gibson's grandfather.

The two champions faced each other.

"Now," concluded Sally. "Who got Merko's money—the tall woman or Fred Gibson?"

Sally wore a smile of triumph as she looked at Encyclopedia.

The tool shed was still. The boys looked at their shoes. Had Sally beaten them again? Had Encyclopedia met his master?

Encyclopedia had five short minutes to solve the brain-twister.

Slowly the minutes ticked away. One . . . two . . . three . . . four . . .

Encyclopedia stirred on his orange crate. He opened his eyes. He smiled at Sally.

"You told it very cleverly," he said. "I nearly said the wrong person. But the answer is really quite simple."

Encyclopedia rose to leave. "The Great Merko's money went to Fred Gibson."

WHY DID ENCYCLOPEDIA SAY THAT?

(Turn to page 125 for the solution to
"The Case of Merko's Grandson.")

The Case of the Explorer's Money

"You haven't touched your breakfast, dear," said Mrs. Brown. "Is something wrong?"

"I'm not hungry," replied Chief Brown. "I'm worried."

"About a case?" asked Encyclopedia.

"Chief Walker of Glenn City wants me to help him recover fifty thousand dollars," said Chief Brown.

"Wow! Did someone rob a bank, Dad?"

"No, the money belonged to Sir Cameron Whitehead, who died last month. He was the famous Arctic explorer."

"Arctic—let's see," said Mrs. Brown. "That means just the North Pole region and not the South Pole area, doesn't it?"

"Yes, that's right," said Chief Brown. "Sir Cameron never went to the South Pole."

"But he made eleven trips to the North Pole," said Encyclopedia.

"Sir Cameron retired to Glenn City three years ago," said Chief Brown. "The money was stolen last month while he lay sick and dying. The Glenn City police still haven't found a clue."

Chief Brown drew a heavy breath. "Chief Walker of Glenn City thinks I can work a miracle. He expects me to capture the thief *presto!*"

"Why can't you?" asked Mrs. Brown. "You have a helper."

Chief Brown grinned. "Want to help, Leroy?"

"Go with you? Boy, would I!" exclaimed Encyclopedia. "I'll telephone Sally Kimball and tell her to look after the detective agency for the day."

Chief Brown went over the case during the half-hour drive to Glenn City.

The fifty thousand dollars had been stolen from a safe in the library of the explorer's home. The police believed the thief had hidden the money somewhere in or around the house, expecting to come back for it later.

The reason for this belief was simple. Anyone could get into Sir Cameron's house. But no one, including the servants, could leave the grounds without being searched by guards.

"Sir Cameron liked visitors," said Chief Brown. "However, he was afraid that someone might steal part of his famous Arctic collection. Ah, here's the estate just ahead."

Encyclopedia saw a large brick house and broad lawns enclosed by a high steel fence. A stream of people was entering by the main gate.

"Sir Cameron died the day after the theft," said Chief Brown. "All of his belongings—his house, his furniture, and his Arctic collection— are being auctioned today."

"Does Chief Walker think the thief will try to slip the money out in the crowd?" asked Encyclopedia.

"Yes, and there aren't enough policemen in the state to watch everyone here today."

As his father parked the car, a big man waved.

"That's Chief Walker. I'll be with him till the sale starts at ten o'clock," said Chief Brown. "Suppose we meet at the front door at ten minutes of ten."

Encyclopedia nodded and glanced at his watch. It was nine o'clock. That gave him fifty minutes to find the fifty thousand dollars!

The boy detective considered the thief's problem.

He could get into the house. But he could not get out of it without being searched by the guards. So after breaking open the safe, where would he hide the money?"

Burying it in the ground would take too long. And someone was sure to see him. Then there was the risk of coming back later to dig up the money.

"The money has to be hidden where no one would think of looking," decided Encyclopedia.

He wandered from room to room. Men and women were examining every stick of furniture. Drawers were pulled out. Cabinet doors were opened. Wives argued with husbands about how much to bid for a chair or table or desk when the sale began.

Nobody screamed. Nobody fainted. Nobody opened a drawer or door and discovered fifty thousand dollars!

Encyclopedia edged up to a piano. Quickly he lifted the lid. Inside was only more piano. He searched on.

At nine-thirty he reached a long room. This was Sir Cameron's private museum. A sign above the door read:

Objects and Animals
From Sir Cameron Whitehead's
50 Years of Exploration
In the Lands of the Far North

In the center of the long room a life-like polar bear stood reared upon its hind legs. Eight little penguins formed a ring at the bear's feet.

More stuffed animals lined one wall. There were a wolverine, an Arctic fox, a caribou, a walrus, and other animals from the North Pole region.

The wall opposite the stuffed animals was hung with articles of Eskimo life: clothing, tools, weapons, and a sled made of driftwood with ivory-tipped runners.

The other two walls of the museum were covered with photographs. Most of them showed Sir Cameron bundled up against snow and ice.

It was ten minutes before ten o'clock. Encyclopedia hurried to meet his father at the front door.

When Chief Brown arrived, he was frowning.

"I'm afraid it's hopeless," he said. "The Glenn City police have gone over every inch of the house and grounds. Somehow, the thief must have got past Sir Cameron's guards with the money."

There were animals from the North Pole.

"No, the money is still here, Dad," said Encyclopedia. "I think this is what happened. The thief waited till other visitors came to see the dying Sir Cameron. The thief went into the house with them bearing gifts.

"While the other visitors were in Sir Cameron's bedroom, the thief waited in the living room," went on Encyclopedia. "Once alone, he broke open the safe, stole the money, and hid it in the—"

IN THE WHAT?

(Turn to page 126 for the solution to
"The Case of the Explorer's Money.")

The Case of the Muscle Maker

Cadmus Turner stopped and glared at the large tree outside the Brown Detective Agency. His lips curled.

"Arrahhrrr!" he snarled.

He crouched, circled to his left, and attacked without warning. He threw both arms about the tree and began wrestling it.

Encyclopedia had never seen Cadmus so full of fight. He hurried out to the sidewalk for a ringside view.

The bout lasted a minute—till Cadmus's pants fell down. He let go of the tree at once.

"It's a gyp!" he hollered. "I've been robbed."

"It looked like a fair fight till your pants

quit," said Encyclopedia. "Next time you tussle the timber, tighten your belt first. You'll win for sure."

"I can't tighten my belt," replied Cadmus. "The ends don't meet any more. I drank four bottles of Hercules's Strength Tonic. I'm ready to bust."

Encyclopedia eyed Cadmus's stomach. It was swollen out like the start of a new continent.

"I should have been able to tear that tree off its roots," said Cadmus.

"Because you drank four bottles of Hercules's Strength Tonic?" asked Encyclopedia.

"Yep," said Cadmus. "Only the stuff doesn't work. I was supposed to feel like Hercules. Instead I feel like a fat slob. And I'm out two dollars!"

"I might get your money back," said Encyclopedia, "if I can prove the tonic is a fake."

"You're hired," said Cadmus. "But I spent all my cash on those four bottles of wish-water. I'll have to pay you later."

Encyclopedia agreed to take the case on faith. Considering the blown-up condition of Cadmus's stomach, it was more an act of mercy than a business deal.

The boys biked to an unused fruit stand on Pine Drive. Cadmus had bought the bottles there earlier that morning.

"Two big kids were setting out boxes of the tonic," said Cadmus. "They told me if I became their first customer, I could have four bottles for the price of two."

"You couldn't say no to a bargain like that," commented Encyclopedia with understanding.

At the fruit stand, a large crowd of children was assembled. Bugs Meany and his Tigers had pushed their way to the front.

The two big boys were about to start the sale. Encyclopedia recognized one of them. He was Wilford Wiggins, a high school dropout. Wilford had more get-rich-quick ideas than tail feathers on a turkey farm. The other boy, a husky youth, was a stranger.

"He's Mike O'Malley," said Cadmus, "from Homestead."

"He looks like he's from Fort Apache," said Encyclopedia. Mike's suit, though it fit perfectly, was wrinkled enough to have gone through an Indian war.

"Gather 'round," shouted Wilford Wiggins. He waved a bottle of Hercules's Strength Tonic. "Gather 'round."

His partner, Mike O'Malley, dropped to the ground and began doing push-ups like a trip-hammer.

"Would you believe Mike weighed only one hundred pounds a year ago?" asked Wilford. "They called him Ribs."

Mike jumped up and removed his suitcoat and shirt. Bare chested, he made muscles in all directions.

"In one short year," bellowed Wilford, "Mike gained a hundred pounds of solid muscle! A miracle, you say? Yes, that's what Hercules's

Bare chested, Mike made muscles in all directions.

Strength Tonic is—a miracle. The same secret miracle tonic can build a mighty body for each and every boy here today—if," he added hastily, noticing Cadmus and his stomach—"if taken as directed."

Mike was wriggling his huge chest muscles. The battleship tattooed over his heart rolled and pitched.

"See that battleship?" asked Wilford. "Why, a year ago it was nothing but a rowboat! Ahah, hah, hah!"

Bugs Meany held his nose at the joke. "How come you have to sell this wash on the street?" he demanded. "If it's so good, you could sell it in stores."

"A fair question, friend," said Wilford. "I'll give you an honest answer. We need money. We're broke."

Wilford held up Mike's wrinkled suit coat.

"Take a look at this suit coat," Wilford said. "Old and shabby, isn't it? Mike's worn it for two years. Why? Because he didn't think about spending money on himself. He thought only of the powerful body he was going to give every skinny, weak-kneed little shrimp in America!"

Wilford put down the suit coat. He picked up a bottle of Hercules's Strength Tonic again.

"Every cent we had went into developing Mike's wonderful tonic," Wilford continued. "We need money to get the tonic into every store in America! It's a crusade! So I'm cutting the price. You can have four bottles—that's all you need—for half the regular price. Four bottles for a measly two dollars!"

"And I thought he was giving *me* a special price," Cadmus said angrily.

"Forget it," said Encyclopedia. "Look at Bugs."

The Tigers' leader was pop-eyed watching Mike's arm muscles lump, jump, and bump.

"How do you take this tonic," Bugs asked eagerly.

"One teaspoonful a day," replied Wilford. "Four big bottles like this one will last twelve months. Then you'll have a build like Mike's!"

"I couldn't wait a year," Cadmus muttered. "So I drank the four bottles one after the other. Maybe the stuff works if you follow the directions."

"It doesn't work," said Encyclopedia. "Mike's muscles and Wilford's big sales talk prove it's a fake!"

HOW DID ENCYCLOPEDIA KNOW?

(Turn to page 127 for the solution to
"The Case of the Muscle Maker.")

The Case of the Stolen Diamonds

Encyclopedia looked up from his book, *Diamonds for Everyone*. His mother stood in the doorway of his room.

"Did you know that diamonds are so hard they're used to drill stone?" he asked.

"I may need a diamond to drill my roast beef," said his mother. "It will be cooked as hard as stone if you don't come to dinner."

"Sorry, Mom," said Encyclopedia. He put the book aside, washed, and hurried to the table. He wanted to talk about diamonds.

His father, however, had a problem.

"The police chiefs from all over the state will be

here next week," said Chief Brown. "They chose Idaville for their yearly meeting."

"Are you worried about how to keep them interested?" asked Mrs. Brown.

"Exactly," said Chief Brown. "Every year there are speeches and more speeches. I want to do something different in Idaville."

"Why don't you have the chiefs solve a crime?" asked Encyclopedia.

"How can I?" asked Chief Brown. "There hasn't been an unsolved crime in Idaville in a year. Thanks to you know who."

"So commit a crime," said Encyclopedia.

"Did I hear you correctly, Leroy?" asked Mrs. Brown.

"I've been reading about diamonds," replied Encyclopedia. "Why not steal a diamond?"

"Mr. Van Swigget, the jeweler, has a diamond necklace," said Chief Brown. "It's worth fifty thousand dollars. Would you like to steal it for me?"

Encyclopedia shook his head and smiled.

"Make believe the necklace is stolen, Dad," he said. "Give the police chiefs all the clues. Then let them try to solve the case."

"Sort of a test, eh?" said Chief Brown thoughtfully. "By golly, you may have something there."

Between the roast beef and the butterscotch pudding, Chief Brown decided to put on the unusual event. Encyclopedia worked out the crime before going to bed.

In the morning his father went to see Mr. Van Swigget. The jeweler agreed to play a part in the make-believe crime. In fact, he was delighted to have a chance to test the best police brains in the state.

So it was that five days later thirty chiefs of police gathered in Mr. Van Swigget's office. Encyclopedia stood in the front of the room beside his father.

Mr. Van Swigget pretended to seem very upset.

"A diamond necklace was stolen this morning," he said. "It is insured for fifty thousand dollars. But money can't replace such a treasure!"

"Pardon me," said one of the chiefs. "What is that necklace on your desk, sir?"

Mr. Van Swigget lifted a necklace from his desk for all to see.

"This," he said, "is a copy of the stolen diamond necklace. As you can see, it is perfect in every way. Only it is made of glass. The thieves didn't bother with it. They knew it wasn't the real diamond necklace."

"Do you believe then that someone in your own store had a hand in the theft?" asked a chief.

"Yes, I do," answered Mr. Van Swigget. "The two necklaces are kept together in a safe when not on display. Had the thieves been unsure of which was the diamond necklace, they would have taken both. But they took only the real necklace."

Near Encyclopedia, one chief whispered to another: "Someone must have told the thieves which was the real necklace."

Mr. Van Swigget stood up. "Now, gentlemen," he said. "Please follow me. I shall show you how it happened."

From the office Mr. Van Swigget led the way into the hall. The floor of the hall was covered with stone. At the end of the hall was a marble staircase.

"The diamond necklace and the glass copy are kept in the safe on the second floor," said Mr. Van Swigget. "Shortly after ten o'clock this morning, I was bringing the fake necklace down to my office. Suddenly two masked men came charging up at me."

Mr. Van Swigget climbed the stairs. At the top he turned around. He started down, holding his hands before him. He was pretending to carry the glass necklace.

"One of the masked men grabbed the glass necklace," went on Mr. Van Swigget. "He fingered it, cursed, and threw it to the floor. At gunpoint the pair forced me back upstairs. I had to open the safe and give them the diamond necklace."

Mr. Van Swigget reached the bottom of the stairs.

Mr. Van Swigget pretended to carry the glass necklace.

"Gentlemen," he said to the police chiefs. "That is what happened. Are there any questions?"

"Are you sure that it would be impossible to tell the glass necklace and diamond necklace apart?" asked a chief.

"Not at a glance," answered Mr. Van Swigget.

Another chief asked, "Who knows about the glass copy besides yourself?"

"My store manager, Mr. Evers, and my secretary, Mrs. Zunser," answered Mr. Van Swigget. "They can tell the two necklaces apart. But they have been with me for twenty years. I trust them completely."

The chiefs had no further questions. Chief Brown stepped next to Mr. Van Swigget.

"In the showroom to your left you will find pencils and paper," said Chief Brown. "I ask you to write down your solution."

"Gosh, Dad," said Encyclopedia as the police chiefs passed into the showroom. "Do you think we made it too easy?"

"We'll soon find out," said his father. "But no

matter how many solve the case, it has made a big hit with everyone."

An hour later Chief Brown finished looking through the answers.

"You didn't make the case too easy," he told Encyclopedia. "Only four of the thirty chiefs named the person behind the theft and told where the diamond necklace could be found."

DO YOU KNOW?

(Turn to page 128 for the solution to
"The Case of the Stolen Diamonds.")

The Case of the Super-Secret Hold

The heart of Bugs Meany was filled with a great longing.

It was to knock Encyclopedia flatter than an elephant's instep.

Bugs hated being outsmarted by the boy detective. But whenever he felt like throwing a punch, he remembered Sally Kimball.

Sally was the prettiest girl in the fifth grade. It wasn't her face, however, that the toughest Tiger remembered. It was her fists.

Sally had done what no boy under fourteen had even dreamed of doing. She had outfought Bugs Meany.

Bugs told everyone that Sally had hit him with

a few lucky punches. Nobody believed his story, including Bugs himself. He thought she had hit him with a milk truck.

Because of Sally, Bugs never bullied Encyclopedia. Sally was the detective's junior partner.

"Bugs hates you more than he hates me," Encylopedia said as the partners sat in the Brown Detective Agency one afternoon. "You can be sure he'll try to get even."

Sally agreed. "He's like a thermometer in hottest Africa," she said. "He's always up to something."

Just then Duke Kelly, one of Bugs Meany's Tigers, entered the garage. He put twenty-five cents on the gasoline can. "Bugs wants you," he said.

"He wants to *hire us?*" gasped Sally.

"No, he wants you to come to the judo show this afternoon," said Duke. "The twenty-five cents will pay for your time."

Encyclopedia and Sally exchanged questioning glances.

"The judo show starts at two o'clock in the junior high school gym," said Duke.

"Judo?" Encyclopedia repeated half to himself. "The gentle art of self-defense?"

"Judo is the art of using your opponent's strength against him," said Duke, "or her."

With that he departed, grinning slyly.

"Bugs has more up his sleeve than his elbow," said Encyclopedia thoughtfully. "But I'm curious."

"So am I," said Sally. "Let's find out."

The junior high school gym was already filled with boys and girls when the detectives arrived. Coach Richards, who ran the summer sports program, spoke briefly. He explained the aims of judo.

Then four men from the Idaville Judo Center took places on the mat in the middle of the floor. They wore white trousers and a loose jacket bound at the waist by a knotted belt. For half an hour they demonstrated holds, locks, throws, and escapes.

After the children had stopped clapping, Coach Richards spoke again.

"Judo is not only for grown-ups," he said. "Three of our own junior high school students will now show you what they have learned in two short weeks."

Bugs Meany and two of his Tigers, Spike Larsen and Rocky Graham, trotted onto the mat. They wore the same white costumes as the men.

"Gosh, he's really good," said Sally as Bugs began flipping Spike and Rocky to the mat like baseball cards.

"They know how to fall without getting hurt," said Encyclopedia. "But the throws are an act. Bugs couldn't toss Spike and Rocky if they didn't let him."

After a whirlwind five minutes, the Tigers lined up and bowed. Coach Richards stepped forward to thank them.

Bugs held up his hand. "I'm not finished," he said.

Coach Richards moved back, surprised.

Bugs repeated the grip on Rocky.

Spike strode toward Bugs. He stopped within a foot of his leader.

Bugs shot a hand to Spike's throat. When he pulled the hand away, Spike fell over on his back and did not move.

Bugs repeated the grip on Rocky. He, too, fell over on his back and lay unmoving.

"You just saw my super-secret hold," announced Bugs. "I completely knocked out Rocky and Spike. But I didn't hurt them. If I really wanted to, though, I could break their necks for life."

Rocky and Spike stirred. They crawled off the mat shaking their heads.

The gym had grown silent. All eyes were on Bugs.

"Now you're asking yourselves, 'Where did Bugs learn this terrible hold?'" he continued. "I'll tell you. I wrote to a famous professor in Japan for the secret."

Bugs strutted up and down the mat. "A lot of you have heard about a certain girl who is supposed to have licked me," he went on. "Now you know I wasn't trying. I could have put her in the hospital, only I'm a gentleman."

His meaning was clear, and all the children understood. Bugs was challenging Sally to a rematch, then and there! If Sally refused to fight, or if she were beaten, Bugs would rule the neighborhood. The Brown Detective Agency would be powerless to halt his bullying.

A small boy near Sally pleaded, "Don't fight him. He could *kill* you!"

But Encyclopedia whispered into Sally's ear. As she listened, her lips tightened. "Super-secret hold, phooey!" she snorted. A moment later she was on the mat.

Bugs turned white. He had thought to scare her. Now *he* was the one who was scared.

There was nothing for him to do but fight. He reached for Sally's throat and took a thump in the stomach.

Fortunately for Bugs, his two-week course in judo had taught him how to fall. Sally's fists gave him plenty of practice. Eventually he lay on his back and refused to get up.

"I can't go on," he wailed. "I hurt my back lifting a big box this morning."

"He must have hurt his head," thought Encyclopedia, "to believe anyone would fall for his super-secret hold!"

WHY DIDN'T ENCYCLOPEDIA BELIEVE THE HOLD?

(Turn to page 129 for the solution to "The Case of the Super-Secret Hold.")

The Case of the Stolen Money

Police officers across America were asking the same question.

Why did everyone who broke the law in Idaville get caught?

Idaville looked like many seaside towns its size. It had two delicatessens, three movie theaters, and four banks. It had churches, a synagogue, and lovely white beaches. And it had a certain red brick house on Rover Avenue.

In the house lived Idaville's secret weapon against lawbreakers—ten-year-old Encyclopedia Brown.

Mr. Brown was chief of the Idaville police force. He was proud of his men. But he was not too proud to get them help.

Whenever Chief Brown came up against a case that no one on the force could solve, he knew what to do. He went home and ate dinner.

Before the meal was over, Encyclopedia had solved the case for him.

Chief Brown wanted to tell the world about his only child—to announce over satellite television, "My son is the greatest detective who ever shot a water pistol!"

But what good would it do? Who would believe that the mastermind behind Idaville's spotless police record was only a fifth-grader?

Encyclopedia never let slip a word about the help he gave his father. He didn't want to seem different from other boys his age.

But there was nothing he could do about his nickname.

Only his parents and teachers called him by

his real name, Leroy. Everyone else called him Encyclopedia.

An encyclopedia is a book or set of books filled with facts from A to Z—just like Encyclopedia's head. He had read more books than anyone in Idaville, and he never forgot what he read. His pals swore that if he went to sleep before thinking out a problem, he stuck a bookmark in his mouth.

Not all his father's most difficult cases happened in Idaville. Friday evening, for instance, the dinner table conversation turned to a mystery in another town.

"Bill Carleton, the Hills Grove chief of police, telephoned me this morning," said Chief Brown. "He has a robbery on his hands that's got him worried."

"Isn't Hills Grove up in Canada, dear?" asked Mrs. Brown.

"It's in northern Canada," answered Chief Brown. "Even during the summer the temperature sometimes drops below freezing."

"The Idaville police department is certainly famous," said Mrs. Brown proudly. "Imagine a call for help from Canada!"

"What was stolen, Dad?" asked Encyclopedia.

"Ten thousand dollars," said Chief Brown. "The money was taken three days ago from the safe in the home of Mr. and Mrs. Arthur Richter."

Chief Brown put down his soup spoon.

"I have all the facts from Chief Carleton," he said. "But I'm afraid I still can't help him find the thief."

"Tell Leroy," urged Mrs. Brown. "He's never failed you yet."

Chief Brown grinned at his son. "Are you ready?" he asked, taking a notebook from his breast pocket. He read what he had written down.

"*Last Friday Mr. and Mrs. Richter, who have lived in Hills Grove three years, flew to Detroit for the weekend. Before leaving, they gave a key*

He had just stepped through the front door when he heard a noise in the study.

*to their empty house to a friend, Sidney Auk-
land, in case of an emergency. On Saturday,
Aukland entered the house."*

"Was it an emergency?" asked Mrs. Brown.

"No," replied Chief Brown. "The weather
had turned cold. It had dropped below freezing.
Aukland said he wanted to be sure there was
enough heat in the house."

Chief Brown read again from his notebook.

*"Aukland said he entered the house Saturday
morning at ten o'clock. He had just stepped
through the front door when he heard a noise in
the study.*

*"He called out, 'Who's there?' and opened the
study door. Two men were at the safe. They
attacked him. He says he didn't have a chance
once they knocked off his eyeglasses. Without
them, he can't see six inches in front of himself.*

*"The two men tied him up, he says. It wasn't
until an hour later that he worked himself free
and called the police."*

"Did Mr. Aukland get a look at the two men

while he still wore his eyeglasses?" asked Mrs. Brown.

"Yes," replied Chief Brown. "He says that if he sees them again, he'll recognize them."

"Then what is the mystery?" exclaimed Mrs. Brown. "Why did Chief Carleton telephone you for help, dear?"

"He suspects Aukland," said Chief Brown. "He thinks Aukland stole the money and made up the part about the two men. But he can't prove Aukland is lying."

Mrs. Brown glanced at Encyclopedia. As yet the boy detective had not asked his one question —the question that always enabled him to break a case.

Encyclopedia had finished his soup. He was sitting with his eyes closed. He always closed his eyes when he did his hardest thinking.

Suddenly his eyes opened.

"What was the temperature in the house, Dad?" he asked.

Chief Brown looked at his notebook.

"Aukland says that the house was comfortably warm when he entered it. After finding his eyeglasses and calling the police, he checked the reading. It was seventy degrees."

"Leroy . . ." murmured Mrs. Brown. Disappointment was in her voice.

She was so proud when Encyclopedia solved a mystery for his father before she served the main course. But sometimes she had to wait until dessert. This looked like a dessert case.

"What is important about heat?" she asked.

"Not any heat, Mom," said Encyclopedia. "The heat in the house."

"I don't follow you, son," said Chief Brown.

"The house was too hot for Mr. Aukland to have seen two men robbing the safe," answered Encyclopedia. "He made them up."

HOW DID ENCYCLOPEDIA KNOW?

(Turn to page 130 for the solution to
"The Case of the Stolen Money.")

The Case of the Skunk Ape

Bugs Meany had one dream in life. It was to get even with Encyclopedia.

Bugs hated being outsmarted all the time. He dreamed of punching Encyclopedia in the mouth so hard that his eyes would be looking for his teeth.

But Bugs never threw a punch. Whenever he felt like it, he remembered Encyclopedia's junior partner, Sally Kimball.

Sally was not merely the prettiest girl in the fifth grade. She had done what no boy under twelve had thought was possible.

She had knocked Bugs Meany goofy.

Whenever they fought, Bugs ended on the

ground, mumbling about the price of yo-yos in China.

Because of Sally, Bugs had quit bullying the boy detective. He never stopped trying to get revenge, however.

"I don't know whom Bugs hates more, you or me," Encyclopedia told Sally. "He'll never live down the lickings you gave him."

Before Sally could answer, Gus Sarmiento rushed into the detective agency. His mouth was open wide enough to swallow a watermelon sideways.

Gus was Idaville's leading boy cello player. Actually, he had first started learning to play the violin. Because of his flat feet, he had switched to the cello. The violin was smaller, but the cello was played sitting down.

"I—I saw it!" he wailed at the detectives. "The Skunk Ape! It reached into my bedroom window!"

The Skunk Ape was Idaville's Abominable

Snowman—a creature supposedly half man and half ape.

"I don't believe in Skunk Apes," said Sally. "Did you smell it?"

"I smelled the carpet," answered Gus. "I was so scared I fell on my face." He let out a moan at the memory.

"A hairy arm reached in and grabbed my empty cello case," he said.

"Ha!" said Sally. "A musical Skunk Ape. This I want to see."

Encyclopedia wished Sally weren't always so brave. But he dared not show a yellow streak. He followed her and Gus to Gus's house.

"I was practicing on the cello when I saw the arm," said Gus. "I always practice . . . between . . . two and three o'clock. . . ."

His voice trailed off. He had halted outside his bedroom window. In a spot of soft earth was a huge footprint.

Encyclopedia's scalp twitched. "This is my

most hair-raising experience since I pulled off my turtleneck sweater," he joked weakly.

"I smell a rat, not a Skunk Ape," said Sally. "Doesn't Wilma Hutton live near here?"

"Three houses down the block," answered Gus.

"She's Bugs Meany's cousin," said Sally. "And she plays the cello!"

Without another word, the three children headed for Wilma's house.

"Look!" said Gus, pointing. A cello case lay among some trees at the side of the garage.

As Gus lifted the case, a car came up the driveway. Wilma Hutton jumped out. She hurried toward the house, taking tripping little steps because of her tight skirt. All the while she screamed, "Police! Police!"

The front door swung open. Out charged Bugs Meany. Behind him was Officer Carlson.

"There's your Skunk Ape, officer!" cried Wilma. "As I drove up, those kids were putting the costume in that cello case."

Gus laid the cello case on the ground and opened it.
Inside was an ape costume. The smell made him stagger.

"That's a dirty lie!" exclaimed Sally.

"Better open the case, Gus," said Officer Carlson.

Gus laid the cello case on the ground and opened it. Inside was an ape costume. The smell made him stagger.

"What died in there?" gagged Bugs.

"Your brain," snapped Sally. "This is a frame-up!"

Bugs clenched his fists and snarled, "May a giant clam bite you on the nose."

"May a sandbag fall on your head," retorted Sally.

"Cool it, you two," said Officer Carlson. "Bugs reported that the Skunk Ape has been frightening his cousin Wilma for days. So I came over to watch for it."

"Wilma can't take much more," Bugs said to the policeman. "She's an artist on the cello. Artists are very high-strung and nervous. That's why they picked on her."

"Oh, that's rich!" said Sally. "She's seventeen

and a date with Frankenstein would be laughs. You're just trying to get even, Bugs Meany!"

"They knew Wilma's parents are off in Europe," went on Bugs. "Poor girl, she's all alone in this big house. A shock like seeing a Skunk Ape can ruin her career."

"What about mine?" howled Gus.

Officer Carlson waved his hand as a sign for the children to be quiet. "We can get to the bottom of this. Is that your cello case, Gus?"

"It looks like mine," replied Gus. "But a lot of cases look like mine."

"Well, it certainly isn't *mine*," declared Wilma.

She went to her car and opened the trunk. She lifted out a cello case.

"I've been in Glenn City playing the cello," she said. "When I arrived home, I saw these kids among the trees with the Skunk Ape costume. When they saw *me*, they shoved it into the cello case fast."

"Wilma and Bugs are in this together," Sally

whispered angrily to Encyclopedia. "I wish I could prove it!"

"You don't have to," replied Encyclopedia. "I can."

WHAT WAS THE CLUE?

(Turn to page 131 for the solution to
"The Case of the Skunk Ape.")

The Case of the Dead Eagles

In all the world there was no place like Idaville, U.S.A.

Idaville looked like many other seaside towns. It had beautiful beaches, three movie theaters, and four banks. It had churches, synagogues, and two delicatessens.

What made Idaville different was a red brick house at 13 Rover Avenue. For there lived Encyclopedia Brown, America's Sherlock Holmes in sneakers.

Because of Encyclopedia, no one in Idaville

—child or grown-up—got away with breaking the law.

Encyclopedia's father was chief of the Idaville police. People all over the world, including China, thought he was the smartest police chief in history.

Chief Brown knew better.

Whenever he came up against a case that no one on the force could crack, he put on his cap and went home to dinner. Before the meal was over, Encyclopedia had solved the case.

Chief Brown would have liked to shout from atop the stone heads carved into Mount Rushmore: "My son belongs here!" But what good would it do?

Who would believe him? Who would believe that the mastermind behind Idaville's war on crime was ten years old?

So Chief Brown kept secret the help he got from his only child.

Encyclopedia never said a word, either. He didn't want to seem different from other fifth graders.

But there was nothing he could do about his nickname. He was stuck with it.

Only his parents and his teachers called him by his real name, Leroy. Everyone else in Idaville called him Encyclopedia.

An encyclopedia is a book or set of books filled with all kinds of facts from A to Z—like Encyclopedia's head. The boy detective had read more books than anyone in Idaville. When he breathed fast, his pals swore they could hear pages turning.

Encyclopedia's quick mind was in demand wherever he went. Not only did he solve cases at the dinner table, but often he was called upon to clear up a mystery when he least expected.

Take, for example, the night he and Charlie Stewart were camping overnight in the state park. They had just pitched their tent when they heard a gunshot.

"Gosh," exclaimed Charlie. "That wasn't far away!"

Encyclopedia threw a log on the fire. He pretended that he hadn't heard a thing.

"It can't be a hunter," reasoned Charlie. "Hunters aren't allowed near the campgrounds."

Encyclopedia slid a marshmallow onto a stick and turned it above the fire. Charlie stared at him in surprise and disappointment.

"Don't you think we ought to *do* something?" Charlie said. "I mean, somebody might have been murdered. "

At times like this, Encyclopedia wished he had never become a private detective.

"Catching a murderer isn't like recovering a stolen bike," he said. "A murderer can stop a person's growth in a terrible hurry."

"But somebody might be hurt and need your help," insisted Charlie.

Encyclopedia sighed. "All right, let's go."

The boys walked through the woods, following a path that led in the direction of the gunshot. After a quarter mile, they reached a clearing. At the far end was a cliff about forty feet high and seventy feet wide.

Encyclopedia suddenly stepped to the edge

Encyclopedia dropped to one knee beside a golden eagle.
It was dead.

of the path. He dropped to one knee beside a golden eagle. It was dead.

"This explains the gunshot," he said, feeling anger and sorrow over the senseless killing.

He looked about the clearing. The setting sun seemed to be resting atop the cliff. He had to shade his eyes before he saw the nest. It was in a cottonwood snag halfway up the cliff.

He pointed out the nest to Charlie. Then he said, "I'll bet Mike Bailey is in the park."

"What has Mike to do with the eagle?" said Charlie.

"Don't you remember last year?" asked Encyclopedia.

A year ago, two golden eagles had built a nest in a cottonwood snag lower down on the same cliff. Soon afterward, both birds were shot during the night.

"About nine o'clock, an hour before the shooting, a scoutmaster noticed Mike Bailey standing on this path," said Encyclopedia. "Mike carried a rifle."

"The scoutmaster could have been mistaken," said Charlie. "It was dark."

"No, there was enough light," replied Encyclopedia. "The moon was full."

Charlie scratched his head. "I wonder about that new nest," he said softly. He walked to the cliff and inched his way up. After a hard struggle, he got his chin above the nest.

"There are two eggs inside," he called down.

The news made finding the mysterious hunter more important than ever. The eagle lying near the path was male. The shot that killed him probably had frightened off his mate. Once she recovered, she would return to hatch the eggs.

"We've got to find the hunter before he shoots the mother eagle, too," said Encyclopedia.

The boys had only one lead—Mike Bailey. He was sixteen and rode a motorcycle. It was dark when they found him at campsite 32.

He had pitched his tent and was reading a

hot-rod magazine by the light of the kerosine lamp. Encyclopedia made out a green motorcycle behind the tent. A rifle lay against the black leather seat.

"Going hunting tonight?" inquired Encyclopedia.

"Naw, I just keep the gun handy," said Mike. "I might see a rattlesnake."

"I don't like guns," said Charlie. "Hunting is cruel unless you need food. And killing wildlife for fun is like murder."

"Oh," said Mike. "You're one of those mouthy kids who believes guns should be outlawed."

"I believe we should have better laws to control guns," said Charlie.

"A gun doesn't shoot by itself," replied Mike sharply. "A gun does what its owner makes it do. Don't control guns, kid. Cure the bad owners."

"You can say the same nonsense about automobiles," said Encyclopedia.

Mike stiffened. "Nonsense? Just what do you mean?"

"An automobile does what its owner makes it do," said Encyclopedia. "So while you're curing bad owners, get rid of all automobile laws— speed limits, traffic signals, drivers' tests, fines, and jail terms."

"Move on, wise guy," growled Mike.

Encyclopedia stood his ground. "A golden eagle was shot in the clearing by the cliff less than an hour ago," he said. "If you shot it, your rifle will still smell of powder."

"Take one step nearer my rifle and I'll break your leg," warned Mike.

"Last year two eagles were shot in the same clearing," said Charlie. "A scoutmaster saw you studying their nest earlier that night."

"So I heard," said Mike. "I was out walking —and I had my gun along in case I saw rattlesnakes. I stopped to admire the full moon, which was right above the cliff. I didn't notice the nest, and I didn't shoot any eagles!"

"You can't help where the moon is," said Encyclopedia. "But you can help lying!"

WHAT WAS MIKE'S LIE?

(Turn to page 132 for the solution to
"The Case of the Dead Eagles.")

The Case of Mrs. Washington's Diary

The Idaville flea market was open every Saturday in the summer. It was held in the vacant field behind the library. The vendors sold everything from secondhand furniture to old sets of china and silver.

Encyclopedia and Sally were moving slowly down one of the aisles, checking out things in the different booths. They passed leather-bound books and old maps of different states.

"There has to be something here," said Sally. "I'll know it when I see it."

"Don't worry," said Encyclopedia. He turned over a cut-glass bowl.

"That's easy for you to say," said Sally. "You're not the one whose mother is having a birthday tomorrow. You're not the one who still doesn't have the perfect present."

"True," said Encyclopedia. "I'm also not the one who waited till the last minute to shop for her."

"I know, I know," said Sally. "Don't remind me. I'm sure I'll find something. My mother loves American history. Around here, there's plenty of history, though most of it is a bit dusty and crumpled. That only proves that it's old."

They passed a booth featuring cast-iron pots and pans hanging on a string. They were jet black and encrusted with a layer of hardened grease.

"These look very old," said Encyclopedia.

"I don't think that kind of history would

appeal to her so much," said Sally. "Let's keep looking."

The booths were laid out in rows, and the detectives carefully went up and down each one. A couple of times they stopped to look at something closely, but there was always a problem of one kind or another.

They had come about three quarters of the way through the market. Sally was beginning to get a little nervous when they saw a high school boy with a booth of his own. A few younger kids were looking at some old toys on his table. There were three yo-yos, some tops, and a wooden chess set that somebody's dog had chewed.

"Step right up," said the boy. "My name's Jack. Jack Higginbottom. I've got a lot of treasures here from my attic. My family has lived in Idaville a long time, so there's plenty to see."

"I didn't know kids could rent space here," said Sally.

"Oh, sure," said Jack. "Everybody's welcome."

Sally picked up a brass letter opener. "Do you have anything really old?" she asked. "Anything historical?"

"I do," said Jack. He opened an old box. It was filled with papers. They were all yellowed and brown around the edges. "I hadn't taken these out before," he explained, "because I didn't want the wind blowing them around."

"Those do look old," Sally said.

"More than two hundred years old," said Jack. "You're looking at pages from the diary of George Washington's mother."

The other kids at the table all stopped what they were doing to listen.

"Her name was Mary Ball Washington," Jack continued, "and she was quite a lady. Born in 1708, she was the second wife of George's father, Augustine. They got married in 1730."

"That's all true," said Encyclopedia.

"Of course it is," said Jack. "Mary, as I like to call her, had a strong opinion of herself. Women in those days, however, weren't allowed to speak their minds, and so she kept a diary. Now, if I had the whole thing, it would be worth a lot of money, but I only have a few pages."

"That sounds perfect," said Sally.

"I have to admit," said Jack, "that most of the pages are concerned with everyday things like chores and life on the farm. By far the best page is the one she wrote the day after George was born."

"What does it say?" asked Sally.

"I'll read it out loud," said Jack. "If you don't mind, I'll handle it myself. The page is pretty delicate." He carefully looked through the papers in the box. "Ah, here it is. Now, it's not a long entry—which is understandable considering that Mary was still recovering from giving birth. These are her words:

I am so impressed looking at little George lying in his cradle. Augustine and I have a feeling he is destined for great things. Why, I wouldn't be surprised if someday he grew up to be president. I only hope I live long enough to see it.

"That's amazing," said Sally.

"Believe or not," Jack added, "she actually did live that long. Mary Ball Washington died in 1789, a few months after her son George was inaugurated the first president of the United States."

"That's true," said Encyclopedia. "I'm sure she was very proud."

Sally could barely contain her excitement. "That's the one I want! I just hope I can afford it."

Jack smiled. "I'm sure we can work out something. I want that page to find a good home."

"My mother will be so excited," said Sally.

"That's the one I want! I just hope I can afford it."

"Right, Encyclopedia? Isn't it just perfect?"

Encyclopedia took a long look at Jack. "I cannot tell a lie," he said finally. "The diary is a fake."

WHY WASN'T ENCYCLOPEDIA FOOLED?

(Turn to page 133 for the solution to
"The Case of Mrs. Washington's Diary.")

The Case of the Hit-Run Car

Encyclopedia and Sally were walking on a quiet street in downtown Idaville when they heard a screech of tires.

Around a corner roared a blue car. Inside were two men. They looked scared.

The car raced down the block and turned onto Ninth Street.

"They're in a mighty big hurry," said Encyclopedia.

"The driver should be arrested before he kills someone," said Sally angrily.

It had been a peaceful afternoon until then. The detectives had just visited Benny Breslin at Mercy Hospital. Benny's tonsils had been removed.

Suddenly they heard a woman shouting. They ran to Jefferson Place, the street from which the blue car had come.

A woman was standing near the sidewalk. She was shouting at the top of her lungs. "Call an ambulance! Call the police!"

A man lay by a parked car. He was holding his back. His face was twisted with pain.

As if in answer to a prayer, an ambulance sped up. Its lights were blinking and its siren screamed.

The woman stepped into the middle of the street and threw up her arms.

"Stop!" she shouted. "Stop!"

Parked cars narrowed the one-way street, and the ambulance driver could not steer around the woman. He slammed on his brakes.

"Lady, get out of the way!" he pleaded. "We're on a call!"

"Take this man to the hospital," she insisted. "He's been hit by a car!"

The driver tried to argue. He had no time

The woman stepped into the middle of the street and threw up her arms.
"Stop!" she shouted.

to stop. "A man on Bradley Square has suffered a heart attack," he said.

The woman held her ground in the middle of the street. "What's the matter with you? This man's hurt!"

The injured man protested. "Let them answer their call," he said. "Mercy Hospital is only two blocks away. I can make it."

"Don't you try!" scolded the woman. "Crazy drivers! Crazy ambulances!"

By now a large crowd of men and women had gathered to watch. They seemed to side with the excited woman.

"Okay, okay, lady, you win," the ambulance driver said, shaking his head. "This could cost me my job, but I guess there is room."

He nodded to his partner and both men got out of the ambulance, their white uniforms bright spots of comfort. They opened the back doors and reached for a wheeled stretcher.

"Heck, I don't need that," said the injured man.

"Yes, you do," said the woman. "The blue car knocked you six feet. I saw it. Oh, I wish I'd got the license number!"

So did Encyclopedia. He had glimpsed only the last part—008.

The two men in white were carrying the stretcher when more sirens sounded. Four police cars halted behind the ambulance.

Chief Brown leaned out of the first car. "Move that ambulance to one side," he commanded.

As the ambulance was being moved, Chief Brown spied Encyclopedia. "What are you doing here, Leroy?" he called.

"We were visiting Benny Breslin at Mercy Hospital," replied Encyclopedia. "This man was struck down by a speeding car."

"Did you see it happen?"

"No," said Encyclopedia. "But I'm pretty certain I saw the car that hit him."

"Are you chasing it?" asked Sally.

"Chasing robbers," said Chief Brown. "The First City Bank was held up ten minutes ago. The bank teller who phoned the station was still so scared she didn't know how many robbers there were. She remembered only that they wore masks and long black capes."

The ambulance had pulled into an open parking space. Chief Brown sent the other police cars on to the bank.

"The hit-run car might be the getaway car," he said. "The bank is only six blocks from here. The robbers would come this way to dodge heavy traffic. What did the car look like?"

"It was a blue four-door Chevrolet, with two men in it," said Encyclopedia. "The last three numbers of the license plate are oh-oh-eight."

"That will help," said Chief Brown. "Who saw the accident?"

"I guess that woman—and the man on the stretcher."

Chief Brown spoke with the woman and the man. He returned to the police car and used the two-way radio.

Meanwhile, the men in white were lifting the injured man into the ambulance. They had strapped him down and were gently rolling him in feet first. Encyclopedia could see the top of his head clearly. It was bald, with cuts that were bleeding slightly.

Encyclopedia thought about the man's head. He thought about the blue car and the men in white. He thought about the woman who had stopped the ambulance.

Chief Brown had finished talking on the radio.

"You're our best witness," he said to Encyclopedia. Neither the injured man nor the woman even recalls how many doors the blue car had. I'm afraid the robbers will take a lot of time to catch."

"No, Dad," said Encyclopedia. "You can make an arrest right now."

WHAT DID ENCYCLOPEDIA MEAN?

(Turn to page 134 for the solution to
"The Case of the Hit-Run Car.")

The Case of the Secret Pitch

Idaville looked like any other town of its size —from the outside.

On the inside, however, it was different. Ten-year-old Encyclopedia Brown, America's Sherlock Holmes in sneakers, lived there.

Besides Encyclopedia, Idaville had three movie theaters, a Little League, four banks, and two delicatessens. It had large houses and small houses, good schools, churches, stores, and even an ugly old section by the railroad tracks.

And it had, everyone believed, the best police force in the world.

For more than a year no one—boy, girl, or grown-up—had got away with breaking a single law.

Encyclopedia's father was chief of police. People said he was the smartest chief of police in the world and his officers were the best trained and the bravest. Chief Brown knew better.

His men were brave, true enough. They did their jobs well. But Chief Brown brought his hardest cases home for Encyclopedia to solve.

For a year now Chief Brown had been getting the answers during dinner in his red brick house on Rover Avenue. He never told a soul. How could he?

Who would believe that the guiding hand behind Idaville's crime cleanup wore a junior-size baseball mitt?

Encyclopedia never let out the secret, either. He didn't want to seem different from other fifth-graders.

There was nothing he could do about his nickname, however.

An encyclopedia is a book or set of books filled with facts on all subjects. Encyclopedia had read so many books his head held more facts than a library.

Nobody but his teachers and his parents called him by his real name, Leroy. He was called Encyclopedia by everyone else in Idaville.

Encyclopedia did not do all his crime-busting seated at the dinner table. During the summer he usually solved mysteries while walking around.

Soon after vacation began, he had opened his own detective business. He wanted to help others.

Children seeking help of every kind came to his office in the Brown garage. Encyclopedia handled each case himself. The terms of his business were clearly stated on the sign that hung outside the garage.

One morning Speedy Flanagan, the shortest fast-ball pitcher in the Idaville Little League, walked into the Brown Detective Agency. He wore a face longer than the last day of school.

"I need help," he said, side-arming twenty-five cents onto the gasoline can beside Encyclopedia. "What do you know about Browning?"

"Nothing, I've never browned," replied Encyclopedia. "But once at the beach I tanned something awful, and—"

"I mean Robert Browning," said Speedy.

"The English poet?"

"No, no," said Speedy. "The American League pitcher, Robert *Spike* Browning."

Even Encyclopedia's Aunt Bessie knew of Spike Browning. He was the ace of the New York Yankees' pitching staff.

"What do you want to know about him?" asked Encyclopedia.

"Do you know what his handwriting looks like?" asked Speedy. "I made a bet with Bugs Meany—my bat against his—that Bugs couldn't get Spike Browning to buy a secret pitch for a hundred dollars."

"Whoa!" cried Encyclopedia. "If I understand you, Bugs bet he could sell Spike Browning a special way to throw a baseball?"

"Right. Bugs and his father were in New York City the last week in June," said Speedy. "Bugs says he sold Spike Browning his cross-eyed special."

"You'd better explain," said Encyclopedia.

"The pitcher crosses his eyes whenever there are runners on first and third bases," said Speedy. "That way nobody knows where he's looking —whether he's going to throw to first base, third base, or home plate. The runners don't dare take a lead. The secret is how the pitcher can throw the ball some place while staring himself in the eye. Bugs sold the secret. He has a letter from Spike Browning and a check for a hundred dollars!"

"Phew!" said Encyclopedia. "I understand you now. You figure Bugs wrote the letter and the check himself to win the bet and your bat. So do I! Let's go see Bugs."

Bugs Meany was the leader of the Tigers, a gang of older boys who caused more trouble than itching powder in Friday's wash. Since setting up as a detective, Encyclopedia had stopped many of Bug's shady deals.

The Tigers' clubhouse was a tool shed behind Mr. Sweeny's Auto Body Shop. When Encyclopedia and Speedy arrived, Bugs was leading a discussion on how to beat the bubble gum machines around town.

The Tigers' leader broke off to greet Encyclopedia. "Get lost," he said.

"Not until I have a chance to see the letter and check from Spike Browning," said Encyclopedia.

Bugs opened a cigar box and passed Encyclo-

Bugs grinned as Encyclopedia read the letter.

pedia a check and a letter. Encyclopedia read
the letter.

Yankee Stadium, New York

June 31

Dear Bugs:

Your cross-eyed pitch is the greatest thing
since the spitball. I expect to win thirty games
with it this season.

For sole rights to the secret of it, I'm happy
to enclose my check for one hundred dollars.

Yours truly,

Spike Browning

The letter was written on plain white paper.
The check, bearing the same date as the letter,
was drawn on the First National Bank for one
hundred dollars.

"Spike will win fifty games this season," said
Bugs. "And I won one baseball bat from Speedy
Flanagan. So where is it?"

"Where's *your* bat?" corrected Encyclopedia. "Speedy won the bet. You lost. The letter and check are fakes."

"I ought to shove those words down your throat," said Bugs. "But I'm feeling too good about what I did for the great American game of baseball."

Bugs crossed his eyes. Humming to himself, he went into his secret throwing motion. The other Tigers cheered wildly.

"Man, oh man!" sang Bugs. "I invented the greatest pitch since Edison threw out the gas lamp. No smart-aleck private detective is going to walk in here and call me a liar!"

"Oh, yes I am," said Encyclopedia. "Spike Browning never wrote that letter. That check is a worthless piece of paper!"

WHAT MADE ENCYCLOPEDIA SO CERTAIN?

(Turn to page 135 for the solution to "The Case of the Secret Pitch.")

The Case of the Junk Sculptor

Harold Finnegan wore eyeglasses, but none of the children called him "Four Eyes."

They called him "Four Wheels."

He was the only boy in the neighborhood who owned two bikes. He had a new bike for clear days and an old bike for rainy days.

However, he was riding his new bike when, on a rainy morning, he came to the Brown Detective Agency for help.

"Hi, Four Wheels," Encyclopedia said cheerfully.

"Call me Three Wheels," said Four Wheels. "I'm down to a bike and a half."

"Did you have a wreck?" asked Sally.

"No, somebody stole the front wheel of my old bike," he said. "I'm pretty sure the thief was Pablo Pizarro."

"How can you say such a thing?" demanded Sally. "Pablo is no thief. Pablo is a great artist! Pablo has feeling! Pablo has—"

"Pablo has my front wheel," insisted Four Wheels. "He stole it ten minutes ago."

Four Wheels rolled twenty-five cents on the gas can. "I'll need your help to get it back, Encyclopedia."

Encyclopedia took the case despite Sally's angry look. On the way to Pablo's house, Four Wheels told what had happened.

"Last night I started fixing my old bike," he said. "I took it all apart. When I went out to the garage this morning, I saw a boy running off with the wheel."

"You aren't sure it was Pablo?" said Sally.

"I never saw his face," admitted Four Wheels. He glanced at Encyclopedia. "You know what's been going on," he said.

Encyclopedia knew. For the past few weeks things had been disappearing from garages in the neighborhood. Strangely, the things were worthless—junk like broken mirrors, bits of wood, old newspapers, and rusty metal parts.

Encyclopedia had not told Sally, but Pablo had been seen hanging around the garages from which the junk disappeared.

The children reached Pablo's house, and Encyclopedia rang the bell. Pablo's mother leaned out a second floor window and called, "Come in. Pablo's in the attic."

Upstairs, Encyclopedia found the attic door locked. He pounded loudly. After a long moment Pablo opened the door.

"Enter," he said with a sweep of his arm. "Welcome to my studio."

Sally's hand fluttered to her mouth as she gazed upon Pablo. He wore a soft flat hat, a large bow for a necktie, and a dirty smock. "You're dressed just like a real artist!" she gasped in admiration.

"Of course," said Pablo with a careless shrug. "I am at work."

"He must be working at building a junk yard in his attic," thought Encyclopedia.

Junk—anything that stayed put—filled every corner. Some of it stood in newly painted mounds. Most just stood rusting away.

Four Wheels got to the point. "Where's my bicycle wheel?"

"Bicycle wheel?" repeated Pablo.

"The one you stole from my garage this morning!" growled Four Wheels.

"My dear fellow, you are talking rot," said Pablo. "It is true that I collect things to use in making my sculpture. But I do not steal!"

The boy artist walked across the attic.

"This is my newest piece," he said, pointing to a pile of wire clothes hangers, coffee pots, magazines, stove legs, an apple, and an automobile tire. "I shall paint it white and call it *Still Life with Apple*."

"Bravo!" squealed Sally in delight.

"This is my newest piece," Pablo said.

Encyclopedia and Four Wheels, being struck speechless, could only stare.

"I haven't been out of the house today," said Pablo. "So how could I steal a bicycle wheel? I've been sitting right here in this old chair working since breakfast. I got up only to answer your knock."

Encyclopedia studied the old chair. It was pulled close to *Still Life with Apple*. The chair was falling apart, but it looked better than Pablo's sculpture.

Small drops of white paint were splattered over the chair. The boy detective ran his hand lightly over the chair's cool seat and touched a few drops. They were dry.

"I don't see my wheel anyplace," whispered Four Wheels.

"Keep searching," said Encyclopedia. "You could hide a battleship in this mess."

Pablo had begun to show Sally around his studio. She followed him like a puppy and hung on every word.

"Upon finding an object in which something else is suggested, the artist uses his skill to bring the idea to fulfillment," said Pablo.

"Come again?" said Four Wheels from a corner.

The boy artist brought forth a board six feet long. On it were nailed a shovel, a fruit box, two smashed electric irons, a bent fan, and scraps of wallpaper.

"I call it *Man in Search of Himself*," said Pablo.

"It's beautiful!" exclaimed Sally. "It's exciting! It lifts me into a world of new ideas!"

Pablo's chest swelled. "I see you are not a beginner," he said. "You understand that what is important in art has nothing to do with cost, or prettiness, or even—"

"Cleanliness!" called out Four Wheels as he crawled behind a dusty heap of tires and chains.

"Don't pay any attention to him or Encyclopedia," said Sally. "They don't know great art when they see it!"

"Maybe not," said Encyclopedia. "But I know a thief when I see one, and Pablo is a thief!"

WHAT MADE ENCYCLOPEDIA SURE?

(Turn to page 136 for the solution to
"The Case of the Junk Sculptor.")

The Case of the Gym Bag

Saturday morning, Encyclopedia and his father went to the high school to watch a track meet. Baldy Jones and Fleet Fletcher were running for Idaville. Baldy shaved his head because he thought it made him run faster. Every morning before a big meet he could be found in the barbershop with a head full of shaving cream.

Today's track meet was between Idaville and Glenn City. However, the real contest was between Fleet and Baldy. The runners were both seniors at Idaville High School. They were on the same team, but they were fierce competitors.

They ran in the same races and almost always came in first and second.

Saturday was no different. Encyclopedia and Chief Brown were both on the edge of their seats. Baldy won the 100-meter dash. Fleet edged him out in the 200. Fleet took the hurdles. Baldy ran a faster 400-meter race. In between events, the two runners sneered insults at each other.

The Glenn City team took third place finishes in every single race.

Encyclopedia was hoarse from cheering for Fleet and Baldy by the time the meet was over. He and Chief Brown were weaving through the crowd on their way to the parking lot when they heard shouting from inside the locker room.

Inside, Baldy and Fleet were standing, nose to nose, snarling at each other.

"Hand it over," Fleet yelled, "or you'll wish you never got out of bed this morning."

"I will not! It's mine," Baldy yelled.

"That's my gym bag. Now give it back," Fleet demanded. "Or I'll—"

"You'll what? You try anything and I'll twist your legs so far around your head, you can eat with your feet," Baldy said with a snarl.

"Hah!" Fleet spat. "First a thief and now a bully."

"I am not a thief," Baldy said. "Just because I let you win a couple of races doesn't mean I'll let you have my gym bag, too."

A small crowd had gathered around the two boys. Encyclopedia and Chief Brown pushed their way to the front.

"Chief Brown, arrest him!" Fleet said. "He's stolen my stamp collection."

"I'll stamp you!" Baldy threatened, raising the bag over his head. "It'll be a very rare stamp— one that sends you straight into outer space."

"You just try," Fleet yelled, raising his fists. "You'll be sending me postcards from Jupiter and Mars."

Chief Brown stepped between them. "Boys,

calm down," he said. "Save your competition for the track."

Fleet and Baldy stopped yelling, but they continued to glare at each other.

Chief Brown waited for a moment. "Now, tell me what happened—"

Fleet and Baldy both started to talk at once.

"One at a time, please," Chief Brown said, holding up his hands. "Fleet, you go first."

"Why does he get to go first?" Baldy whined.

"Because he's not holding a gym bag over my head," Chief Brown said calmly.

Baldy sheepishly lowered the bag and handed it to the police chief.

"I showered and changed after the meet," Fleet said, pushing his bangs off his forehead. "I left my gym bag on the bench while I stepped into Coach Lewis's office. When I came out, Baldy was leaving the locker room with *my* gym bag."

"It's *my* gym bag," Baldy insisted. "He's just saying it's his because he knows I have my stamp

"*It's my gym bag!*"

collection with me today. It's worth a lot of money."

Chief Brown turned to Fleet. "Can you prove this is your gym bag?"

"I mentioned to a couple of guys that I was heading over to the stamp store after the meet to see about selling my collection. There's a collector in town just for today, and he's interested in some of my rare stamps," Fleet explained.

"Is there any identification in the bag?" the chief asked.

Fleet shook his head. "It's a new bag. I didn't think to add an ID tag."

"I was the one who didn't think to add an ID tag," Baldy said. "I can't prove it's mine, either."

The chief opened the bag and pulled out the contents. He lined up the items on the stairs leading to the locker room. Aside from the stamp collection, protected in a plastic folder, the bag held standard items: a damp towel, soap, deodorant, hair gel, and a clean pair of socks.

Fleet checked his wristwatch and moaned.

"The stamp collector is leaving town at five o'clock. It's already four-thirty."

"I'll have to hang on to the gym bag and the stamp collection until I can identify the owner," the chief said. "I'm sorry, but one of you will have to miss the stamp collector."

"Give Fleet his gym bag, Dad," Encyclopedia said. "If he runs like he did at the track meet, he'll get to the stamp store in time."

HOW DID ENCYCLOPEDIA KNOW THE BAG BELONGED TO FLEET?

(Turn to page 137 for the solution to
"The Case of the Gym Bag.")

The Case of the Champion Skier

Dinner at the Browns' red brick house in Idaville was not like dinner in other homes.

The Browns not only broke bread together. They broke crimes together.

Mr. Brown was chief of police. People everywhere thought that he was the brains behind Idaville's wonderful record of law and order.

Nobody could have guessed the truth. Behind Chief Brown's success was his only child —ten-year-old Encyclopedia.

Chief Brown brought home his hardest cases. Encyclopedia solved them while eating dinner. Since he had begun secretly helping his father, no crook had escaped arrest, and no child had got away with ducking the law.

Chief Brown would have liked to pin a medal on Encyclopedia every time his son solved a case. But what good would it do?

Who would believe that the real mastermind behind Idaville's crime cleanup was a fifth grader?

Besides, Encyclopedia couldn't have stood up under all the medals without getting flat feet.

So Chief Brown said nothing.

Encyclopedia never let slip a word about the help he gave his father. He did not want to seem different from other boys.

However, there was nothing he could do about his nickname.

Only his parents and teachers called him by his right name, Leroy. Everyone else called him Encyclopedia.

An encyclopedia is a book or set of books full of facts from A to Z—like Encyclopedia's brain. He had done more reading than just about anybody in town. His pals said that when he turned a cartwheel, his head sounded like a bookcase falling over.

But one evening Chief Brown brought home a case Encyclopedia couldn't solve during dinner.

Chief Brown explained why. "We don't have any facts," he said.

Mrs. Brown was relieved. "No wonder Leroy can't help you," she said. "What kind of crime is it, dear?"

"Kidnapping," answered Chief Brown. "One of our ambassadors in Latin America has been kidnapped. That's all I've been told. The State Department wants me to fly down and see what I can do."

"It sounds like a top-secret case," said Encyclopedia. "Boy, I wish I could go along!"

"You can," said his father. "The State Department wants my visit to look like a family holiday. So all three of us are going."

The next morning Encyclopedia had his first view of Idaville from the sky.

He couldn't tell the houses of the rich families from those of the poor families, the churches from the synagogues, or the delicatessens from the banks.

Before he had had time to pick out his own house, the jet was flying over the Gulf of Mexico. He opened his book, *Vertebrate Paleontology*. As he reached the last chapter, the jet put down with a light bump.

At the airport the Browns were met by a man in a dark suit. He said he was a chauffeur from the hotel. He loaded their bags into the back of a green car.

As he started the engine, he introduced himself again. He was really Mr. Rico, a police officer.

"The kidnapped man is Mr. Ware, your ambassador here," he said. "We are going to his home now."

On the way, Mr. Rico told Chief Brown all the facts that were known about the case.

Mr. Ware had been kidnapped two days earlier. He had been driving to a hotel in the

At the airport the Browns were met by a man in a dark suit.

mountains for a week of skiing. His empty car had been found in the snow two miles below the hotel.

"Mr. Ware is a champion water skier," said Mr. Rico. "But he had never skied on snow. He wanted to learn."

"Had he ever been to the hotel in the mountains before?" asked Chief Brown.

"No," replied Mr. Rico. "He told no one where he was going except his wife. In fact, he got a room at the hotel under a different name."

"Why did he want to do that?" inquired Mrs. Brown.

"For safety's sake," replied Mr. Rico. "Foreign service has become dangerous here. People who don't like the government have taken to kidnapping foreign officials."

"How much money are the kidnappers asking for Mr. Ware's return?" said Chief Brown.

"The kidnappers never want money," answered Mr. Rico. "They want their friends freed from prison. For Mr. Ware, they are demanding the freedom of forty men being held in prison for crimes against the government."

"How awful!" exclaimed Mrs. Brown. "Kidnapping an innocent man to win freedom for criminals!"

Mr. Rico continued. "The night Mr. Ware disappeared, he gave a birthday party for himself. He was forty-five. He invited six friends. Each brought a gift. They came at eight o'clock and found food, servants, and a note from Mr. Ware. The note said he'd had to leave the city early and for everyone to enjoy the party without him."

"Was there a reason for his missing his own party?" inquired Chief Brown.

"There was a weather report of a snowstorm due that night," said Mr. Rico. "He must have figured that if he stayed for the party, he'd find the mountain roads to the hotel snowbound. So he left the city before the storm."

Mr. Rico stopped the car in front of the ambassador's large house. He unlocked the front door.

On the sofa in the living room were the six birthday gifts.

"I opened them," said Mr. Rico. "I thought there might be a clue among them, but there wasn't."

Encyclopedia and his father looked over the gifts. Each gift had a card bearing the name of the guest who had brought it to Mr. Ware's party.

They were a spear gun from Bill Watson, a can of ski wax from Harry Smith, a face mask from Dan Perske, an air tank from Kurt Haper, a pair of water skis from Marty Benton, and a rubber diving suit from Ed Furgis.

Mr. Rico said, "Mrs. Ware is certain that her husband told no one about the trip to the mountains but herself."

"Mr. Ware must be a proud man," said Chief Brown. "He doesn't want to be seen doing anything until he can do it well."

"Yes," agreed Mr. Rico. "He is a champion water skier. But he didn't want anyone to see him learning to ski on snow and perhaps looking silly. So he kept his trip a secret."

"He *must* have told someone besides his wife," said Chief Brown. "And that someone worked with the kidnappers."

Mr. Rico nodded. "But whom did Mr. Ware tell?"

Chief Brown looked at Encyclopedia.

Encyclopedia whispered, "He told . . ."

WHOM?

(Turn to page 138 for the solution to
"The Case of the Champion Skier.")

Solution to *The Case of Merko's Grandson*

Both the tall woman and Fred Gibson spoke the truth.

Although the Great Merko was not his grandfather, Fred Gibson was the Great Merko's grandson.

The Great Merko, as Encyclopedia realized, was a woman. She was Fred Gibson's *grandmother!*

Solution to *The Case of the Explorer's Money*

The thief brought eight gifts—the penguins. These he stuffed with the money and placed in the museum.

He came back to the house on the day of the sale. He bought the penguins. He expected them to be shipped to him. But the police arrested him instead.

Solution to *the Case of the Muscle Maker*

Wilford Wiggins tried to make the children believe Mike had gained a hundred pounds in one year by drinking Hercules's Strength Tonic.

He also tried to make them believe Mike had been unable to buy a suit because all his money went into developing the tonic.

But the old suit coat still "fit perfectly" on Mike.

If Mike had really gained a hundred pounds in one year, he would have outgrown the suit coat!

When Encyclopedia pointed out this fact to the crowd of children, Wilford had to stop the sale.

And he returned Cadmus's two dollars.

Solution to *The Case of the Stolen Diamonds*

In the test thought up by Encyclopedia, Mr. Van Swigget played the part of the criminal mastermind.

He had hired the masked men to rob him—of the wrong necklace!

Remember how the masked man on the stairway had thrown the supposedly glass necklace away? Had it truly been glass, it would have broken on the stone floor.

But the "glass" copy that the police chiefs saw on Mr. Van Swigget's desk wasn't broken. It was "perfect."

So the necklace on his desk, which had been thrown to the floor, had to be the diamond necklace. Diamonds, being harder than stone, wouldn't have broken on the stone floor.

The masked men had stolen the glass necklace!

Thus in the make-believe theft Mr. Van Swigget not only kept the diamond necklace. He would have collected the fifty thousand dollars' insurance money besides!

Solution to the Case of the Super-Secret Hold

Bugs tried to scare Sally with his super-secret hold.

All the children but Encyclopedia believed that Spike and Rocky were really put to sleep, and that they could have been seriously hurt if Bugs had wanted to hurt them.

Encyclopedia alone saw that Spike and Rocky weren't really knocked out.

He whispered to Sally the reason he knew they were only faking.

Spike and Rocky had fallen over on their backs.

A person who is knocked senseless, or who loses consciousness while standing up, does not fall backward.

He falls forward.

Solution to *The Case of the Stolen Money*

After stealing the money and hiding it in his own house, Mr. Aukland returned to the Richters' house with rope.

He called the police, claiming the rope had been used by two thieves to tie him; before he could free himself the thieves got away with the money.

However, he claimed to have seen them clearly before they knocked off his glasses.

Impossible!

Entering a house heated to seventy degrees—a comfortable temperature—from the outdoors on a freezing day, Mr. Aukland could not have seen anything.

His eyeglasses would have been steamed over!

Thanks to Encyclopedia, Mr. Aukland confessed.

Solution to *The Case of the Skunk Ape*

Bugs got Officer Carlson to wait in Wilma's house during the time Gus always practiced the cello.

Meanwhile, Wilma dressed as the Skunk Ape and stole the cello case. Then she rubbed the costume with rotten eggs, stuffed it into the case, and left the case where it could be easily found.

Bugs knew Gus would run to Encyclopedia for help. When the children found the cello case, Wilma was watching from her parked car. She drove up the driveway and then hurried toward the house in her tight skirt.

Encyclopedia realized that she could not have just come home from playing the cello, as she claimed.

A cello is held between the legs. A woman wears pants or a loose skirt—never a *tight* skirt—to play it!

Solution to *The Case of the Dead Eagles*

Mike said that the year before he had not been looking at the eagles or their nest. He had simply been admiring the full moon, which was "right above the cliff."

Standing on the same path, Encyclopedia and Charlie had seen the setting sun atop the cliff.

So they all had been facing west.

Unfortunately for Mike's alibi, the full moon is never seen in the western sky at night!

Trapped by his own words, Mike admitted killing the three eagles. He promised to spare the mother eagle and her eggs if the boys did not tell on him.

The boys kept their word. Mike kept his.

Solution to *The Case of Mrs. Washington's Diary*

As Encyclopedia knew, it would have been quite a feat for George Washington's mother to write that someday her baby boy would be president. After all, he was born in 1732. At the time, there was no president, and no United States, either. Both of these things only came to be fifty-seven years later, after the Constitution of the United States had been adopted. Washington did become the first president in 1789, and his mother lived long enough to see him inaugurated.

When Encyclopedia informed him of his error, Jack admitted he had made the diary pages himself. He apologized to Sally and offered her anything she wanted in his booth for free. Sally found a nutcracker shaped like Teddy Roosevelt's head and took that instead. Her mother was delighted.

Solution to *The Case of the Hit-Run Car*

The robbers had worn hospital uniforms beneath their black capes and used a stolen ambulance as the getaway car.

They had planned everything—except the mischance of passing an accident.

They could not run over the shouting woman or ignore her pleas without drawing attention to themselves.

Still, they might have got away, but for Encyclopedia. He realized they weren't really ambulance men. They loaded the injured man into the ambulance feet first.

All life-support equipment is stored behind the front seat of an ambulance. So patients are always loaded *head first*!

P.S. Aided by the license plate numbers which Encyclopedia had seen, the police caught the hit-run driver as well.

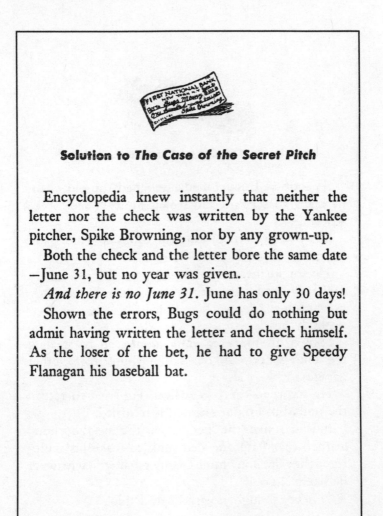

Solution to *The Case of the Secret Pitch*

Encyclopedia knew instantly that neither the letter nor the check was written by the Yankee pitcher, Spike Browning, nor by any grown-up.

Both the check and the letter bore the same date —June 31, but no year was given.

And there is no June 31. June has only 30 days!

Shown the errors, Bugs could do nothing but admit having written the letter and check himself. As the loser of the bet, he had to give Speedy Flanagan his baseball bat.

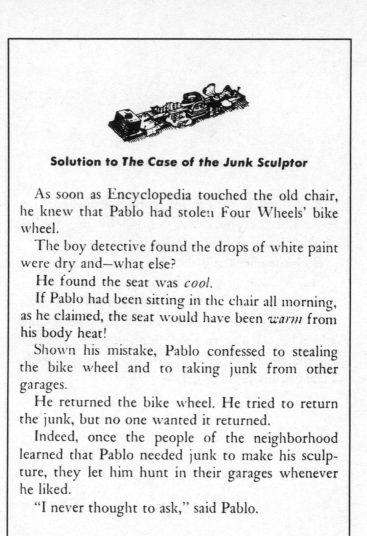

Solution to *The Case of the Junk Sculptor*

As soon as Encyclopedia touched the old chair, he knew that Pablo had stolen Four Wheels' bike wheel.

The boy detective found the drops of white paint were dry and—what else?

He found the seat was *cool.*

If Pablo had been sitting in the chair all morning, as he claimed, the seat would have been *warm* from his body heat!

Shown his mistake, Pablo confessed to stealing the bike wheel and to taking junk from other garages.

He returned the bike wheel. He tried to return the junk, but no one wanted it returned.

Indeed, once the people of the neighborhood learned that Pablo needed junk to make his sculpture, they let him hunt in their garages whenever he liked.

"I never thought to ask," said Pablo.

Solution to *The Case of the Gym Bag*

Baldy lied about the gym bag and the stamp collection. Neither belonged to him. When he overheard Fleet talking about the stamp collector and the value of the stamps, he looked for an opportunity to grab the bag.

When Fleet stepped into the coach's office, Baldy saw his chance. He hadn't counted on getting caught by Fleet.

The items in the gym bag gave Baldy away. He was well known for his shaved head. Baldy had no use for the hair gel in the gym bag. That proved the bag belonged to Fleet.

Fleet made it to the stamp store just in time.

Solution to *The Case of the Champion Skier*

Mr. Ware, the kidnapped man, was a champion water skier who didn't want anyone to know he was learning to ski on snow.

So he told only two persons—his wife and Harry Smith.

Harry Smith was one of the six friends Mr. Ware invited to his birthday party.

Encyclopedia saw that five of the gifts were in keeping with Mr. Ware's known interest in water skiing.

But Harry Smith had brought a gift useful only for skiing on snow—*ski wax!*

The police arrested him. Having given himself away, he told where Mr. Ware was being held prisoner.

Mr. Ware was freed unharmed.

Read the first book in the series!

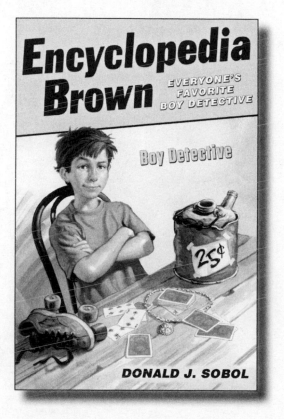

Join Encyclopedia as he solves mysteries involving a bank robbery, missing roller skates, a stolen necklace, and more!

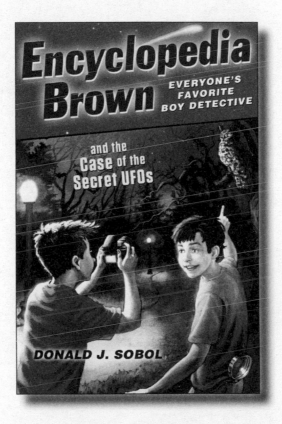

Join Encyclopedia as he solves mysteries
involving a case about stolen stamps, missing
medallions, a shipwreck, and more!

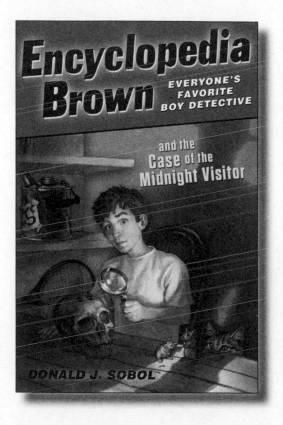

Join Encyclopedia as he solves mysteries
involving a kidnapped millionaire, a
dangerous dog, a famous crook, and more!